I Am Not a Fox

written by **Karina Wolf**

illustrated by **Chuck Groenink**

G. P. Putnam's Sons

On Luca's first day in the city, he went to the park to make new friends. Outside on the gate, he found a list of rules:

NO FERRETS, PARROTS, POSSUM,
RABBITS, WILDCATS, OR IGUANAS.
IF YOU'RE NOT A DOG, KEEP OUT!

Inside, a pack of dogs regarded him.

"You're not a dog," they said. "You're a fox!"

"That's impossible," Luca said. "I chase cats and yip at mailmen and sniff other dogs you-know-where."

The head Doberman snorted. "Any fox can *act* like a dog."

"I have a waggy tail and a whiskery nose," Luca said.

The second-in-command whiffed. "Any fox can look a little like a dog."

"I am not a fox."

"Prove it," said the Doberman.

Luca looked around at all the snouts
and tails and ears and coats.

It was true. He did not look like any
of the other dogs.
So he left.

As Luca walked the city, he found other creatures he looked like.

Luca had a shaggy mane around his neck, but he wasn't a lion. Luca had spindly legs for leaping, but he wasn't a horse. Luca had a fluffy tail that curled when he was nervous, but he wasn't a squirrel.

"I am not a fox," Luca insisted.

A pack of hunting hounds thought Luca was a fox.

They chased him under a bridge, around a pond, and into a fountain.

Luca hid in a museum, where he found a painting of animals who resembled him exactly.

"At last! Dogs like me." But then Luca read the display: They were a skulk of foxes.

"I don't want to be a fox," said Luca. "But it looks like I am one."

That night, Luca looked for
a forest so he could live as a fox.

All he could find was the green at
the center of the city.

There, he made a fox's dinner of salad with
a side of fried worms. It was delicious.

Luca lay under the inky sky and watched the
stars. There are a few good things about being a fox,

At dawn, Luca raced up a hill, chasing a bluebird for breakfast.

At the top of the hill, he lost the bird.

But there he found himself nose-to-nose with three other foxes.

"A pack of foxes!" Luca exclaimed. "Can I join you?"

The foxes looked at Luca, and Luca looked at them.

"But you are not a fox," the foxes said.

"I am a fox! Everyone thinks so. I have a pointy nose. And a brushy tail."

"Any dog can *look* a little like a fox," the foxes replied.

"People run away from me because I'm a wild animal," Luca said.

"Any dog can scare a person," sniffed one fox. "But people do not scare you."

"And why are you looking for company? We don't live in groups," the foxes said. "That's a very doggish behavior."

And the three foxes scattered because a girl was approaching.
"I have always wanted a pet fox," said the girl, who found
Luca all alone. "You should come home with me."
As a dog, Luca knew he shouldn't go
home to a stranger's apartment. But as a
wild animal, Luca could do as he pleased.

"What do you look like?" the little girl asked when she got a good view of him. "You are not a fox."

"No, I am *not* a fox," Luca practically shouted.

"You have the face of a fox. And the long legs of a deer and the mane of a lion. I don't know what you are."

"No one knows," Luca said.

Then the girl showed Luca all the other
unusual creatures who lived in the city:
a woman with a neck like an ostrich,

a snake that was a man's necktie,

a boy who wore a gorilla suit,

and a boy who wore an iguana on his shoulder.

The girl held Luca in her arms. "You are the most wonderful mystery I've ever seen. You shall be my mystery dog."

SPORTING DOGS

The next day at the dog park, Luca fluffed out his flame-colored fur and displayed his dog tag proudly.

The chief Doberman stopped them at the gate. "If you're a dog, where's your pack? All dogs have other dogs, or at least a person to play with."

Before, Luca did not have a person or a pack, but now he had the girl.

Inside, the pack of dogs began to whisper, "What kind of dog is this? That's a fox."

Luca smiled his foxiest smile and puffed out his coat.

"I am not a fox," Luca said. "I'm a mystery dog. The very best kind. And you can call me Luca."

For Misha, Violet, Ellis, Sophia,
Merci, Briana, and Walker.
—K.W.

For Hazel, Dolf, and Ruby.
—C.G.

G. P. Putnam's Sons
an imprint of Penguin Random House LLC
375 Hudson Street, New York, NY 10014

Library of Congress Cataloging-in-Publication Data
Names: Wolf, Karina, author. | Groenink, Chuck, illustrator. | Title: I am not a fox / by Karina Wolf ; illustrated by Chuck Groenink. | Description: New York, NY : G. P. Putnam's Sons, [2018]
Summary: When Luca arrives in a city, the dogs tell him he is a fox and not welcome in their park, so he sets out to discover which he is, dog or fox. | Identifiers: LCCN 2017048862 |
ISBN 9780399174506 (hc) | ISBN 9780399548574 (epub fxl cpb) | ISBN 9780399548598 (kf8/kindle) |
ISBN 9780399548581 (epib/nook) Subjects: | CYAC: Identity—Fiction. | Dogs—Fiction. |
Foxes—Fiction. | City and town life—Fiction.
Classification: LCC PZ7.W81918 Iaam 2018 | DDC [E]—dc23
LC record available at https://lccn.loc.gov/2017048862
Manufactured in China by RR Donnelley Asia Printing Solutions Ltd.
ISBN 9780399174506
10 9 8 7 6 5 4 3 2 1
Design by Eileen Savage. Text set in Adelle. The art was drawn in Photoshop with customized brushes and scanned smudges and splatters.